jJ Fic

Copyright © 1997 by Nord-Süd Verlag AG, Gossau Zürich, Switzerland.
First published in Switzerland under the title *Evie fliegt nach Afrika*.
English translation copyright © 1997 by North-South Books Inc.

First published in the United States, Great Britain, Canada,
Australia, and New Zealand in 1997 by North-South Books,
an imprint of Nord-Süd Verlag AG, Gossau Zürich, Switzerland.

Library of Congress Cataloging-in-Publication Data is available.
A CIP catalogue record for this book is available from The British Library.
ISBN 1-55858-793-4 (trade binding)
1 3 5 7 9 TB 10 8 6 4 2
ISBN 1-55858-794-2 (library binding)
1 3 5 7 9 LB 10 8 6 4 2
Printed in Belgium

For more information about our books, and the authors and artists
who create them, visit our web site: http://www.northsouth.com

Evie
to the Rescue!
By Hermann Moers
Illustrated by Gusti

Translated by Marianne Martens

North-South Books

New York / London

It was a rainy day—the kind of day to spend indoors. But Evie was tired of being stuck inside.

"Why don't you paint pictures?" asked Mother.

"I don't want to paint pictures," said Evie. "I want to go to the zoo. You promised to take me when you had time," she reminded her mother. "You have time today."

"A promise is a promise," said Evie's mother. And off to the zoo they went!

At the zoo most of the animals were in their houses, hiding from the rain. At the lion house Evie saw a little lion cub snuggled up to his mother.

"Hello, little lion," said Evie. "How are you?"

"I'm cold," the lion cub replied, burrowing deeper in his mother's warm fur.

"You should go to Africa," suggested Evie. "Africa is the land of the lions. It's nice and warm there."

Evie couldn't stop thinking about the poor, cold little lion cub. She was still worrying about him when she went to bed that night.

In the middle of the night, Evie's mother woke her up. "Evie, someone is here to see you."

The little lion cub from the zoo was standing in the doorway! Evie rubbed her eyes.

The lion cub scampered across Evie's room and climbed up on her bed.

He settled down next to Evie and announced proudly, "I just slipped between the legs of the zookeeper and followed your tracks here. I was hoping you would show me the way to Africa—you know, the land of the lions," he said.

"You certainly are brave," said Evie. "I'll see what I can do."

"I have to go away for a little while," Evie told her parents the next morning. "I'm taking the little lion cub to Africa."

"To Africa?" asked Evie's father. "Won't that be dangerous?"

"Not at all," replied Evie. "He's a lion, so nothing can happen to us. All I need is some stale bread, my car seat from the car, and my baby car seat from the attic."

Evie and the lion cub went to the park. With the car seats strapped to their backs, they looked like a couple of tortoises.

At the pond, Evie shook the stale bread into the water. "Hello!" she called.

A huge swan approached. He quickly gobbled up the bread.

"Would you please take us to Africa?" asked Evie.

The swan was happy to help, so Evie and the lion cub strapped the car seats to the swan's back and climbed on.

The swan flew high over the mountains.
"Yippee!" shouted Evie. "We'll be in Africa in no time!"
"I'll just keep my eyes shut for now," said the lion cub. "This is making me dizzy."

"I've never been to Africa," said the swan. "How will I know when we're there?"

"You'll know right away," said Evie. "It will be warm, and there will be wild animals everywhere."

"Then we must be there already," said the swan, and he started to land.

They landed on a beautiful beach. Evie and the lion cub romped happily on the sand.

"It's certainly nice and warm here," said Evie. "But do you see any wild animals?"

"That animal over there looks pretty wild," said the swan.

Evie laughed. "That's a donkey! We're at a campsite. It reminds me of the one my parents took me to in Italy. Maybe that's where we are, 'cause I don't think we're in Africa yet."

So they continued on their journey. As they crossed the sea, the air became warmer and warmer.

"I think we're closer to Africa," said Evie happily. "Oh, look! There's the desert. Would you land, please?"

Evie was thrilled by all the sand in the desert and immediately started to build a sand castle.

The little lion cub was *not* thrilled. "There isn't one single lion here," he pouted. "Let's keep going."

They continued flying, and when at last they saw green trees and a big blue lake, they landed.

The swan plunged into the water to wash the sand out of his feathers. Evie and the lion cub walked into the jungle, and soon they were surrounded by all sorts of animals.

"Look at all the animals for you to play with!" Evie said. Then she saw that the lion cub was crying. "What's wrong?" she asked.

"I'm the only lion here," the cub replied. "I thought this was supposed to be the land of the lions."

"Don't cry," said Evie. "We'll keep looking."

So on they flew. Before long they looked down and saw a whole pride of lions lying in the sun. When the swan landed next to them, with Evie and the cub on his back, the lions just yawned lazily.

"Excuse me," said Evie. "I've brought you a little lion cub. Please take good care of him."

The lions nodded and swished their tales in a friendly way.

The little lion cub thanked Evie and kissed her good-bye, and then rushed over to play with the other cubs.

As evening fell, Evie and the swan took off, heading for home. Evie settled happily into her car seat and fell asleep.

When she woke up, she was in her own bed.

"Wake up, sleepyhead," said Evie's mother.

"I took the poor cold little lion cub back to Africa," Evie said sleepily. "He was so happy! Or was it just a dream?"

"I don't know," said her mother. "But even if it was only a dream, I think the lion cub will be just as happy staying at the zoo with his mother—especially since today it's sunny and much warmer. It's such a nice day, how would you like to go back to the zoo and see if your friend is there?"